Annabel Again

by Janice Boland
pictures by Megan Halsey

Dial Books for Young Readers · New York

Published by Dial Books for Young Readers
A Division of Penguin Books USA Inc.
375 Hudson Street
New York, New York 10014

Design by Nancy R. Leo
Printed in Hong Kong
First Edition
1 3 5 7 9 10 8 6 4 2

Library of Congress Cataloging in Publication Data
Boland, Janice.
Annabel again / by Janice Boland ; pictures by Megan Halsey.—1st ed.
p.   cm.
Summary: A little pig with a desire to find a new place to live asks
a bird, a frog, and a cat why their homes are unique.
ISBN 0-8037-1756-3 (trade).—ISBN 0-8037-1757-1 (library)
[1. Pigs—Fiction. 2. Home—Fiction. 3. Animals—Fiction.]
I. Halsey, Megan, ill. II. Title.
PZ7.B635849Ap 1995   [E]—dc20   94-189   CIP   AC

The full-color artwork was prepared using pen and ink, watercolor, dyes,
pastels, and colored pencils. It was then scanner-separated and reproduced
as red, blue, yellow, and black halftones.

To Steven and Beth
J. B.

For Jodi again
M. H.

Annabel rolled out of the mud puddle. She took a deep breath. The air was so sweet.

"I don't want to stay here anymore, Mama," she said. "I want to find someplace new to live. I want to find someplace different. I want to find someplace exciting!"

"Of course you do, dear," said Mother Pig. "It's springtime."
She sighed as Annabel trotted away.

Annabel danced into the garden. She saw a bird in a little plum tree.

"I'm looking for someplace new to stay," said Annabel.

"Come stay with me," tweet, tweet, tweeted the bird. "I've just built a new nest. Come see. Come see," she sang.

Annabel peered through the branches and leaves at the bird's nest.

"That is new!" she cried. "I will stay with you."

Annabel tried to climb into the little plum tree, but it bent beneath her. Down, down, down it went. Then *TWANG!* it snapped back up. And the nest flew through the air.

"Oh, dear. Oh, dear," twitted the bird. "I'll build us another nest, Annabel."

"No thanks!" said Annabel, looking up at the bird. "A nest in a tree is not for me." She turned on her heel and off she went.

Annabel skipped over the hill to the pond. She saw a frog in the reeds.

"I'm looking for someplace different to stay," said Annabel.

"Come stay with me," croak, croak, croaked the frog. "I live on a lily pad."

"That is different!" cried Annabel. "I will stay with you."

"Follow me. Follow me," called the frog as he leaped into the air.

Annabel scrunched herself up. She leaped into the air and landed on top of the frog.

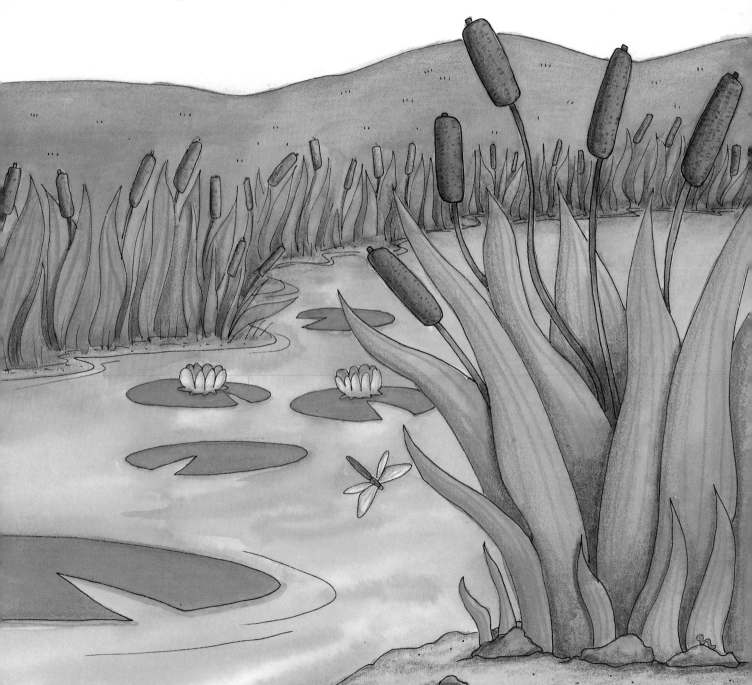

SPLOOSH! Down sank the frog. Down sank the lily pad. Down sank Annabel, down, down, down to the bottom of the pond.

"Oh, dear. Oh, dear," sputtered the frog, popping up in the water. "I'll find us a different lily pad, Annabel."

"No thanks!" said Annabel, swimming to shore. "A pad on a pond is not for me." She shook the water out of her ears and hurried away.

Annabel pirouetted across the meadow. She was going to find someplace exciting! She could feel it in her heart.

Annabel saw a cat dozing on a stone wall.

"I'm looking for someplace exciting to stay," said Annabel.

"Come stay with me," purr, purr, purred the cat. "I live in a secret place full of wonderful things. It's hidden deep in the woods."

"That is exciting!" cried Annabel. "I will stay with you!"

"Come this way," whispered the cat.

Annabel's feet tingled as she followed the cat down a twisted path through the dark woods.

Annabel's heart pounded as she followed the cat into an old forgotten barn. This *was* exciting!

Inside, the barn was filled with cobwebs, shadows, and spooky noises.

A bat flit, flit, flitted past Annabel's nose. A mouse squeak, squeak, squeaked across Annabel's toes. An owl whoo, whoo, whooed, then swooped over Annabel's head.

"Isn't this exciting?" meowed the cat, leaping and twitching his tail.

"It's too exciting," said Annabel. "I'm leaving."

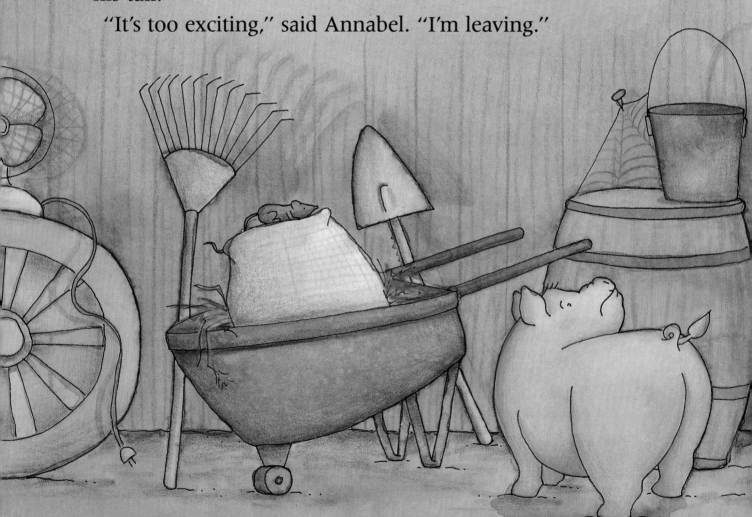

Annabel raced through the woods. She ran across the meadow. She rushed past the pond and over the hill, and burst out of the garden.

"I'm back, Mama!" she cried.
"That's wonderful, dear," said Mother Pig. "I'm so glad."
"You are?" squealed Annabel.
"Yes, I am," said Mother Pig.

Annabel jumped into the mud puddle.
"This is the best place to be," she cried.
"Of course it is," said Mother Pig. "It's home."